22.79

Wetlands

Wetlands

Andrew Donnelly

THE CHILD'S WORLD®, INC.

Library of Congress Cataloging-in-Publication Data
Donnelly, Andrew.
Wetlands / by Andrew Donnelly.
p. cm.
Includes index.
Summary: A brief introduction to wetlands, their appearance,
location, and plants and animals that live there.
ISBN 1-56766-466-0 (lib. reinforced : alk paper)
1. Wetlands—Juvenile literature.   [1. Wetlands.]   I. Title.
QH87.3.D48   1998
578.768—dc21   97-30408
CIP
AC

Photo Credits

© Art Gingert/Comstock, Inc.: 24
© 1997 Bill Lea/Dembinsky Photo Assoc. Inc.: 29
© Cameron Davidson/Tony Stone Images: 10
© 1994 Darrell Gulin/Dembinsky Photo Assoc. Inc.: 13
© David Davis: 15
© 1993 DPA/Dembinsky Photo Assoc. Inc.: 16
© 1995 DPA/Dembinsky Photo Assoc. Inc.: 26
© Gary Brettnacher/Tony Stone Worldwide: 9
© 1994 George E. Stewart/Dembinsky Photo Assoc. Inc.: 23
© 1996 Jim Battles/Dembinsky Photo Assoc. Inc.: 20
© 1994 John Gerlach/Dembinsky Photo Assoc. Inc.: 6
© 1993 Mark J. Thomas/Dembinsky Photo Assoc. Inc.: 19
© Randy Wells/Tony Stone Images: 30
© 1993 Russ Gutshall/Dembinsky Photo Assoc. Inc.: 2
© 1994 Terry Donnelly/Dembinsky Photo Assoc. Inc.: cover

On the cover...

Front cover: This Wisconsin wetland is full of tall grasses.
Page 2: This wetland in Alaska is full of lily pads.

Table of Contents

Walking along a country road, you come to a place where the ground gets soggy. As you continue walking, you notice shallow water and tall weeds. A little farther on, you can see many kinds of plants and animals. Everything in this place seems to live in or near the water. What kind of place is this? It's a wetland!

What Do Wetlands Look Like?

A wetland is a special kind of place, or **environment**. An environment is a type of land that has certain kinds of water, plants, and animals. The land in a wetland environment is flooded with water for most of the year. The wetland air is cool and moist. Hundreds of plants and animals live in the slow-moving, shallow water.

This wetland in Idaho is full of water. ⇒

There are many different kinds of wetlands. Swamps, bogs, and marshes are all types of wetlands. Wetlands come in different sizes, too. Some are small, like a shallow pond. Others are quite large. The *Florida Everglades* is huge area covered with wetlands. It is almost as big as the state of Delaware!

What Plants Live in Wetlands?

Many wetlands are covered with green, grasslike plants. One of these plants is called the *cattail*. Cattails can grow over six feet tall. They have a fuzzy brown top that looks like a burnt hot dog. If you look closely, you can see what the top is made of—seeds! When the time is right, the seeds break away from the top and fly away in the wind.

Cattails like these are often found in wetlands. ⇒

Instead of grasses, some wetlands have huge trees growing in the wet mud. One of these trees is the *mangrove tree*. Mangroves have huge roots that keep them from falling over in the soft mud. Many animals make their homes in the roots and branches of mangrove trees. The strong roots help keep the wetland mud from washing away during storms.

These *mangrove trees* are growing in a Florida wetland. ⇒

From far away, the water in a wetland looks clear. As you get closer, you can see that the surface is covered with green scum. This scum is actually one of the wetland's most important plants—**algae**. Algae is a tiny plant that floats in the water. A wetland has millions of algae plants. These small plants produce air that people and animals need to breathe.

⇐ This green *algae* is made of millions of tiny plants.

Algae is also an important food for many wetland animals. Snails, insects, and small fish all eat algae. Then larger fish and birds eat the insects and snails.

Even if they don't eat it, all wetland animals need algae. That is because the algae feeds the animals that feed other animals. It is the beginning of the wetland's **food chain**. In a food chain, animals depend on other animals and plants for food.

This heron and turtle are both part of their wetland's food chain. ⇒

What Animals Live in Wetlands?

Wetlands are home to thousands of different animals. If you look in the water, you can find shrimp, crabs, fish, and clams. You can also find turtles and frogs. Ducks and geese float on the water. Beavers, muskrats, and otters swim through the waters of northern wetlands. Alligators swim in the wetlands of the south. Other animals live along the shores.

Many animals that make their homes in wetlands cannot be found anywhere else. Some of these animals are **endangered**, or in danger of dying out. If the wetlands are destroyed, these animals will die.

⇐ These *green frogs* are hiding in wetland plants.

Why Are Wetlands Important?

Wetlands are important for many reasons. They provide homes, or **habitats**, for thousands of animals. They are important sources of food for people. And since wetlands can teach us so much about nature, they are important places to visit and study. Studying wetlands can teach us how to care for many natural areas.

This *white-tailed deer* is getting a drink of wetland water. ⇒

Wetlands also protect other areas of land. That is because they act like huge storage containers. When an area gets a lot of rain, much of the water runs into wetlands. The wetlands hold the water and prevent flooding. Without wetlands, many areas would be flooded every time it rains.

Scientists are finding out that wetlands not only hold water, they clean it as well! The water that enters a wetland is full of dirt and sometimes chemicals. As the water slowly moves through the wetland, the plants and roots act like a screen. The dirt and muck are left behind for the plants and animals to feed on. Wetlands act as a natural water filter!

Where Are Wetlands Found?

There are wetlands in almost every country of the world. But for many years, people destroyed the wetlands. They thought wetlands were dirty, useless places. Many wetlands were drained to make room for farmland, shopping malls, and roads.

Today we know that wetlands are very important places. But in some areas, wetlands are still being destroyed to make room for buildings. As more and more wetlands are destroyed, the plants and animals that live there disappear.

This wetland is beginning to dry up. ⇒

Are Wetlands in Danger?

Many governments now protect wetland areas so people cannot drain them. However, wetlands are still in danger from pollution and garbage. When chemicals and trash collect in the water, wetlands become too damaged for the animals to use. If we are careful to preserve them, we can enjoy our wonderful and valuable wetlands for a long, long time.

⇐ Many types of plants grow in wetland water.

Glossary

algae (AL–jee)
Algae are tiny plants that live on the surface of the water. Many animals like to eat wetland algae.

endangered (en–DANE–jerd)
When something is endangered, it is in danger of dying out. Many wetland animals are endangered.

environment (en–VY–run–ment)
An environment is the land, water, plants, and animals that make up a certain type of area. A wetland is one kind of environment.

food chain (FOOD CHANE)
In a food chain, big animals depend on smaller animals and plants for food. In a wetland, the food chain begins with tiny algae.

habitat (HA–bih–tat)
An animal's habitat is its home. Wetlands provide habitats for many kinds of animals.

Index